THE
FOLLETT

JUST
BEGINNING-TO-READ
SERIES

The
Three
Little
Pigs

The
Three
Little
Pigs

Margaret Hillert

illustrated by Irma Wilde

Follett Publishing Company

CHICAGO

Here is a pig.

Here is a pig.

And here is a pig.

One, two, three.

Three little pigs.

Three funny little pigs.

See my house.

It is a little house.

It is yellow.

Little pig, little pig.

I want to come in.

You can not.

You can not.

You can not come in.

I can puff the house down.

Puff, puff, puff.

Here is my house.

It is a funny little house.

Little pig, little pig.

I want to come in.

You can not.

You can not.

You can not come in.

See me puff, puff, puff.

I can puff the house down.

19

Look here, look here.

My house is a big one.

It is red.

Little pig, little pig.

I want to come in.

Go away.

Go away.

You can not come in.

See me puff.

I can puff.

I can puff the house down.

23

See here, see here.

My house is not down.

I can go up, up, up.

I can go in.

25

Oh my, oh my.

It is funny.

You can not go up.

You can not come down.

And you can not come in.

Follett JUST Beginning-to-Read Books

Uses of these books. These books are planned for the very youngest readers, those who have been learning to read for about six to eight weeks and who have a small preprimer reading vocabulary. The books are written by Margaret Hillert, a first-grade teacher in the Berkley, Michigan, schools. Each book is illustrated in full color.

Children will have a feeling of accomplishment in their first reading experiences with these delightful books that *they can read*.

The Three Little Pigs

The classic nursery story told in just 34 preprimer words with charming illustrations that carry the action of the story.

Word List

7	here		house	**15**	puff
	is		it		the
	a		yellow		down
	pig				
				19	me
9	and	**13**	I		
			want	**20**	look
10	one		to		big
	two		come		red
	three		in		
	little			**22**	go
	funny				away
		14	you		
12	see		can	**25**	up
	my		not		
				26	oh